ABBIE IN STITCHES

Cynthia Cotten
Pictures by Beth Peck

FARRAR STRAUS GIROUX

NEW YORK

SOURCES

Edmonds, Mary Jaene. *Samplers & Samplermakers: An American Schoolgirl Art 1700–1850*.
  New York: Rizzoli International Publications, 1991.

Ring, Betty. *Girlhood Embroidery: American Samplers & Pictorial Needlework 1650–1850*.
  New York: Alfred A. Knopf, 1993.

Rochester (N.Y.) Museum and Science Center. *"Behold the Labour of My Tender Age":*
  Children and Their Samplers, 1780–1850 (catalog accompanying an exhibit,
  April 15, 1983–January 22, 1984).

Text copyright © 2006 by Cynthia Cotten
Pictures copyright © 2006 by Beth Peck
All rights reserved
Distributed in Canada by Douglas & McIntyre Ltd.
Color separations by Embassy Graphics
Printed and bound in the United States of America by Phoenix Color Corporation
Designed by Jay Colvin
First edition, 2006
10 9 8 7 6 5 4 3 2 1

www.fsgkidsbooks.com

Library of Congress Cataloging-in-Publication Data
Cotten, Cynthia.
    Abbie in stitches / Cynthia Cotten ; pictures by Beth Peck.— 1st ed.
      p. cm.
    Summary: Growing up in western New York State in the early 1800s, Abbie would
much rather read than embroider a sampler, which her mother and teacher insist she
do, but she works hard after thinking of just the right picture and saying to include.
Contains facts about education in the early nineteenth century.
    ISBN-13: 978-0-374-30004-3
    ISBN-10: 0-374-30004-6
    [1. Embroidery—Fiction. 2. Schools—History—Fiction. 3. New York (State)—
History—19th century—Fiction. 4. Education—History—19th century.] I. Peck, Beth,
ill. II. Title.

PZ7.C82865Ab 2006
[E]—dc22

                                                                    2004043283

For my mother, Mary Lou Storrs,
who taught me to stitch and gave me my love of books
—C.C.

For Berina, Rachel, Sam, Maddy,
and Anna Rose
—B.P.

On a sunny October day, in a small house in western New York State, Abbie Rogers and her older sister, Sarah, sat making tiny stitches on pieces of homespun linen.

"Why must I do this, Mama?" Abbie asked.

"One day you'll have a home of your own," Mama said. "You'll need to sew household linens and clothes for your family."

"That's plain sewing," Abbie said. "Why do I need to know so many fancy stitches?"

Mama kissed the top of Abbie's head. "To show you're an accomplished young woman."

Abbie frowned. She hated the cloth that bunched and never stayed clean.

"I will not stitch when I'm grown," she said to Sarah. "I'll have books instead of needles and thread, and read as much as I like."

"Books are for boys," Sarah said. "Needlework is for girls."

Sarah loved needlework. Her stitches were always even, and her work was always neat. Last year Sarah had stitched her first sampler—a piece of needlework using many of the stitches she had learned. Mama and Papa had been so proud when she finished it. Mama gave her a little box that held a thimble, a small pair of scissors, and four needles that had come all the way from London. Papa framed Sarah's sampler and hung it on the wall.

The next day was Wednesday, the worst day of the week for Abbie. Every Wednesday after school, Abbie, Sarah, and five other girls walked the short distance from the schoolhouse to the home of Mrs. Elvira Brown for their weekly needlework lesson.

Today, Abbie walked more slowly than the others.

"Walk faster, Abbie," Sarah called from Mrs. Brown's porch. "You'll be late."

Abbie didn't care if she was late. She didn't care whether she got there at all, because today she would start her first sampler.

When they were all seated in the parlor, Mrs. Brown spoke to the youngest girls first. "Liza, Mary, and Jane," she said, looking at the cloth each girl held in a wooden hoop, "your running stitches are beautiful: straight and small and even. You're ready for the cross stitch." She threaded a needle and began to show the girls what to do.

Two years ago, Abbie had learned the running stitch and the cross stitch. Since then she had learned the hemstitch and stem stitch, queen stitch and chain stitch, satin stitch, eyelets, and tiny French knots. No matter how many she learned, though, Mrs. Brown always seemed to have a new one.

"Abbie?" Mrs. Brown touched her shoulder. "Abbie, pay attention. It's time to talk about your sampler."

Mrs. Brown handed each of the bigger girls a piece of tan linen. "Here's the cloth you brought last week. I've drawn the border on it for you to stitch first. After that, you'll work the alphabet, your numbers, a picture, and a saying. Abbie and Lottie, since this is your first time stitching a sampler, your pictures will be simple. Sarah and Becky, I expect you to stitch something more complicated."

Abbie picked out her skeins and threaded her needle. Up and down, in and out went her needle as she began to stitch the border of leaves and berries. Up and down, in and—

"Ouch!"

"Be careful, Abbie," Mrs. Brown said. "Please try not to bleed on the cloth this time."

Every day after school, Abbie sat at home by the front window, working on the border. As the last autumn leaves fell from the trees, she sometimes felt she just couldn't cross one more stitch, so she put her sampler down and read from one of the books on Papa's shelf. But when Mama caught her, she always made her put it back.

"I'm sorry," Mama said, "but stitching must come before books."

By the time the first snow fell, Abbie had finished the border. Next she began stitching the alphabet, first in capital letters, then in small ones. Up and down, in and out. Left to right, right to left.

One Wednesday, Mrs. Brown had to say, "Pay attention, Abbie. You must cross all your stitches in the same direction. Take these out and do them again."

Abbie frowned as she snipped and pulled the tiny stitches out of the coarse linen cloth.

Stitch, snip, pull, try again. Some days, Abbie thought she'd never get it right. Counting threads and making tiny stitches by candlelight made her head ache. Once, when she stuck her finger very hard with the needle, Mama let her sit by the fire with Papa's book of stories by Mr. Washington Irving. "The Legend of Sleepy Hollow" was one of Abbie's favorites.

The first spring blossoms appeared, and some afternoons it was warm enough for Abbie to stitch outside in the garden. She had finished the alphabet and the numbers one through ten. Now it was time for a picture and some words.

What would she stitch?

A house?

She threaded her needle and began to stitch the outline of a red house. Then she remembered the house on Sarah's sampler, a house that looked just like their real one. Abbie's would never look as good as that. She sighed and took the stitches out.

A horse! She would stitch a black horse like the one the headless horseman rode. But the outline of the horse she stitched looked more like a dog, with short legs and big ears. Once again, Abbie sighed and took the stitches out.

"Abbie," Mrs. Brown said one day, "you seem to have fallen behind. The other girls have already begun their pictures."

"I know," Abbie said. "I just can't decide what to stitch."

"Look here, at some of my samplers," Mrs. Brown said. "You could do a flock of sheep or a willow tree or maybe a basket of flowers, like Lottie."

Abbie shook her head. "I want to do something different. Something special for me."

Mrs. Brown smiled. "When you go home today, think about what is important to you."

All that evening, Abbie thought. She wished she could bury her sampler out in the garden and never see it again. The only pictures and words she wanted to see were in the book of poems Grandmother had sent for her birthday last year.

Just before she fell asleep, an idea came to her.

As soon as she got home from school the next day, Abbie began to stitch a picture so simple that her needle fairly flew. Every day after school, she stitched up and down, in and out. When she finally finished, she smiled at the outline of an open book she had stitched on the linen. On the left-hand page was her name. On the right-hand page was the date: April 20, 1822. Beneath the book were these words: *I would rather read.*

Abbie showed her finished sampler to Mama, Papa, and Sarah.

Papa chuckled. Mama frowned. Sarah smiled.

"Abbie, these are not proper words for a sampler," Mama said.

"Is that how you really feel, Abbie?" Papa asked.

"Yes, Papa."

"Then leave it the way it is. It's a fine sampler."

"But what will people say?" Mama asked.

Papa squeezed Abbie's shoulder. "They'll say she's a girl who's not afraid to speak her mind."

When Mrs. Brown asked to see Abbie's sampler, Abbie unfolded the cloth.

"Oh, my," Mrs. Brown said. She hid her mouth behind her handkerchief and gave a little cough.

The other girls crowded around to see Abbie's sampler. Some laughed when they saw it.

Abbie bit her lip. She knew why they were laughing. Traces of red and black showed on the linen where the house and the horse had been. The letters "M" and "W" were crooked. And a big brown bloodstain showed at the bottom.

Mrs. Brown shushed the other girls. "This is a good beginning, Abbie," she said with a smile. "I'm sure your next sampler will be even better. Soon you'll be as good at stitching as you are at reading."

Abbie took her sampler home. Papa hugged her and said he would frame it and hang it right beside Sarah's. Mama kissed her and gave her a little box. Inside was a thimble, a small pair of scissors, and four needles that had come all the way from London.

"Wait, Abbie." Mama gave her something else.

Gulliver's Travels—a book of her very own! And inside the front cover was a bookmark Sarah had stitched.

"Oh, Mama, Papa, Sarah, thank you!" Abbie hugged them all.

Then, carefully putting the little box away, she pulled a chair over by her window, sat down, and began to read.

AFTERWORD

Although Abbie Rogers is a fictional character, she was inspired by a girl I read about when doing research on historical samplers. A book published in 1921 titled *American Samplers*, by Ethel Stanwood Bolton and Eva Johnston Coe, mentioned a sampler stitched around 1800 that said, "Patty Polk did this and she hated every stitch she did in it. She loves to read much more."

I was intrigued by this girl's outspokenness at a time when most samplers dealt seriously, and often depressingly, with duty and death. Nobody I contacted knew the whereabouts of this sampler. Today, many people doubt its existence, saying it might just be a needlework legend.

Countless American girls of the eighteenth and nineteenth centuries stitched samplers for a number of reasons. In those days, sewing skills were important for a homemaker who made her own household linens and clothing for her family. If a girl needed to find work, sewing was a skill that could help her get a job as a lady's maid or a dressmaker. Samplers also served as reference tools. Pattern books were rare, so if a woman wanted to use a certain stitch or design, she could pull out a sampler and refresh her memory.

Some girls learned needlework at home, but more learned in schools. In Abbie's time, it was common for both boys and girls to attend what was called a dame school, in the home of an unmarried woman or a housewife. Parents paid a small amount for their children to attend such a school, where they learned reading, writing, and, often, the basics of sewing and knitting. As the children grew older, boys and girls were usually taught separately, although sometimes in small towns, such as Abbie's, they might still attend school together.

Because many families wanted their daughters to learn more than just reading and writing, private schools known as female academies began to appear. Usually only upper- and middle-class parents could afford to send their daughters to these schools. Besides academic subjects, these girls learned what were known as "accomplishments" —needlework, painting, and music—that would make a girl much more attractive when she became old enough to marry. Abbie's fictional town is small, like many of the towns that began to grow on the frontier of western New York State in the early 1800s, and so does not have a true female academy—just Mrs. Brown, who would have been paid by her students' parents for the needlework lessons she gave in her home.

Some girls probably enjoyed needlework; others—like Abbie—probably hated it. No matter how they felt about it, though, making a sampler was an important part of a girl's education.

723 1885

723 1885